Philipp Winterberg   Nadja Wichmann

ฉันตัวเล็กหรือ?
Am I small?

Text: Philipp Winterberg · Illustrations: Nadja Wichmann · Translation: Philipp Winterberg (English), Universal Translation Studio
Original title: Bin ich klein? · Fonts: Patua One/Arial Unicode · Production: CreateSpace, North Charleston, SC 29406, USA · Printed in
Germany by Amazon Distribution GmbH, Leipzig · Publisher: Philipp Winterberg, Münster · Infos: www.philipp-winterberg.com
Copyright © 2014 Philipp Winterberg · ISBN: 978-1494941079 · All rights reserved. No part of this book may be reproduced,
stored in a retrieval system, or transmitted by any means without the written permission of the author.

นี่คือแทมเมีย
This is Tamia.

ใช่แล้ว!
แน่นอนที่สุด!
Right!
Exactly!

แทมเมียยังตัวเล็กมาก
Tamia is still very small.

ฉันหรือ?
ตัวเล็ก?
Me?
Small?

ฉันตัวเล็กหรือ?
Am I small?

ตัวเล็ก? เธอน่ะเหรอ? เธอตัวเล็กยิ่งกว่าเล็ก!
เธอตัวเล็กกระจิ๋วหริว!
**Small? You? You are smaller than
small! You are teeny-weeny!**

ตัวเล็กกระจิ๋วหริว? เธอ?
เธอตัวกระจ้อยร่อย!
**Teeny-weeny? You?
You are mini!**

เธอตัวเล็กกระจิ๋วหริว หรือ?
Am I teeny-weeny?

ตัวกระจ้อยร่อย? เธอ?
เธอตัวนิดเดียว!
Mini? You? You are tiny!

ฉันตัวกระจ้อยร่อยหรือ?
Am I mini?

ฉันตัวนิดเดียวหรือ?
Am I tiny?

ตัวนิดเดียวหรือ? เธอ?
เธอตัวเล็กจนมองไม่เห็น!
Tiny? You?
You are microscopic!

ฉันตัวเล็กจนมองไม่เห็นหรือ?
Am I microscopic?

ตัวเล็กจนมองไม่เห็นหรือ? เธอ?
เธอตัวใหญ่!

Microscopic? You? You are big!

ฉันตัวใหญ่หรือ?
Am I big?

ตัวใหญ่หรือ? เธอ?
เธอตัวโต!
Big? You?
You are large!

ฉันตัวโตหรือ?
Am I large?

ตัวโตหรือ? เธอ?
เธอตัวใหญ่มาก!

Large? You?
You are huge!

ฉันตัวใหญ่มากหรือ?
Am I huge?

ตัวใหญ่มากหรือ? เธอ?
เธอตัวมหึมา!

**Huge? You?
You are gigantic!**

เดี๋ยวก่อน... ฉันรู้แล้ว!
ฉันเป็นทุกสิ่ง...

**Wait a minute...
I've got it!
I'm everything...**

ตัวเล็กจนมองไม่เห็น!
Microscopic!

ตัวเล็กกระจิ๋วหริว!
Teeny-weeny!

ตัวโต!
Large!

ตัวมหึมา!
Gigantic!

ตัวใหญ่มาก!
Huge!

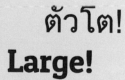

...และถ้าฉันเป็นทุกสิ่ง, ฉันก็ยัง: ดูดี!

...and if I'm everything, I'm also: just right!

More books by Philipp Winterberg

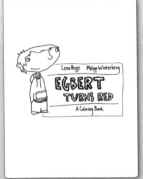

Egbert turns red

Yellow moments and
a friendly dragon...

Print-it-yourself eBook (PDF) Free!

DOWNLOAD » www.philipp-winterberg.com

In here, out there!

Is Joseph a Noseph or some-
thing else entirely?

INFO» www.philipp-winterberg.com

Fifteen Feet of Time

A short bedtime story
about a little snail...

PDF eBook Free!

DOWNLOAD » www.philipp-winterberg.com